Anonymous

Acts of the Board of Education

Anatiposi

Anonymous

Acts of the Board of Education

Reprint of the original, first published in 1874.

1st Edition 2023 | ISBN: 978-3-38250-120-4

Anatiposi Verlag is an imprint of Outlook Verlagsgesellschaft mbH.

Verlag (Publisher): Outlook Verlag GmbH, Zeilweg 44, 60439 Frankfurt, Deutschland
Vertretungsberechtigt (Authorized to represent): E. Roepke, Zeilweg 44, 60439 Frankfurt, Deutschland
Druck (Print): Books on Demand GmbH, In de Tarpen 42, 22848 Norderstedt, Deutschland

ACTS

OF THE

BOARD OF EDUCATION

OF THE

STATE OF ALABAMA.

SESSION COMMENCING NOVEMBER 17, 1873.

MONTGOMERY, ALA.:

ARTHUR BINGHAM, STATE PRINTER.

1874.

SCHOOL LAWS.

No. 1.] AN ACT

To provide for the publication of the School Laws
and proceedings of the Board of Education and
Board of Regents at session of 1873.

SECTION 1. *Be it enacted by the Board of Edu-* Three thousand copies of laws.
cation of the State of Alabama, That the Superin-
tendent of Public Instruction be, and he is hereby
authorized to have published three thousand copies
of the school laws passed at this session of the
Board, and such official circulars as he may deem
necessary.

SEC. 2. *Be it further enacted*, That said Super- Five hundred copies of pro-ceedings.
intendent of Public Instruction be, and he is hereby
authorized to have published five hundred copies of
the proceedings of the Board of Education and
Board of Regents at the present session.

SEC. 3. *Be it further enacted*, That the sum of Compensation to clerk.
one hundred dollars be, and is hereby appropriated
to pay J. H. Francis, Clerk of the Board of Education, for preparing said proceedings for publication,
and the Superintendent of Public Instruction is authorized to certify said sum to the State Auditor,
who shall draw his warrant on the State Treasurer
in favor of J. H. Francis for the same.

SEC. 4. *Be it further enacted*, That the Super- Fifteen copies to each mem-ber of board.
intendent of Public Instruction be, and he is hereby
authorized and required to send by express fifteen

copies of said proceedings to each member of this Board.

Approved Dec. 5, 1873.

No. 2.]   AN ACT

To provide for the payment of County Superintendents of Education.

SECTION 1. *Be it enacted by the Board of Education of the State of Alabama*, That each county superintendent of education shall receive four (4) per centum of the amount allowed on his quarterly requisition upon the Superintendent of Public Instruction for services performed in accordance with law ; he shall also receive three (3) dollars per diem while actually engaged in visiting schools, and in his quarterly requisition he shall make affidavit of the number of days so engaged in visiting schools : *Provided*, That he shall not receive in any one year more than one hundred dollars for such service in visiting schools : *Provided further*, That no county superintendent of education shall receive less than three hundred dollars for his entire services as county superintendent of education and for visiting schools.

SEC. 2. *Be it further enacted*, That no county superintendent of education shall receive any compensation under this act for any requisition made for moneys which are to be paid out of the school fund for any year preceding the scholastic years 1873 and 1874.

SEC. 3. *Be it further enacted*, That the provisions of this act shall apply to the scholastic year 1873 and 1874 and all subsequent years.

SEC. 4. *Be it further enacted*, That all laws and parts of laws in conflict with this act be, and the same are hereby repealed.

Approved December 9, 1873.

Margin notes:

Four per cent of amount allowed on requisition.

Per diem for visiting schools

Proviso.

Not less than $300.

No compensation for years prior to 1873–74.

No. 3.]   AN ACT

Relating to the payment of the salaries of County
   Superintendents of Education for the scholastic
   year 1872–3.

SECTION 1. *Be it enacted by the Board of Edu-*
cation of the State of Alabama, That county superintendents of education shall be paid their salaries
for the scholastic year 1872–3 out of the fund apportioned to their respective counties for that year,
in accordance with the provisions of an act to be entitled "an act to provide for the pay of county
superintendents of education," approved Dec. 14,
1871.
   Approved Dec. 9, 1873.

———

No. 4.]   AN ACT

To provide for the removal of county superintendents of education, and for filling vacancies in the
   same.

SECTION 1. *Be it enacted by the Board of Edu-* Causes of re-
cation of the State of Alabama, That the Superin- moval.
tendent of Public Instruction be, and hereby is authorized to remove any county superintendent of
education for any one of the following causes, to-
wit: For misfeasance or malfeasance in office, for
gross incompetency, immorality or drunkenness.
   SEC. 2. *Be it further enacted,* That the Superin- Vacancies, how
tendent of Public Instruction be, and hereby is au- filled.
thorized to fill any vacancy that may occur in the
office of county superintendent of education caused
by removal, death, resignation or otherwise.
   SEC. 3. *Be it further enacted,* That all laws and
parts of laws in conflict with this act be, and the
same are hereby repealed.
   Approved December 5, 1873.

No. 5.]   AN ACT

To provide a contingent fund.

Appropriation of $1000.

SECTION 1. *Be it enacted by the Board of Education of the State of Alabama*, That the sum of one thousand dollars be, and is hereby appropriated from the general school fund to provide for the contingent expenses of the Board of Education and Educational Department.

SEC. 2. *Be it further enacted*, That the Superintendent of Public Instruction shall certify to such claims and accounts as he shall order paid out of such contingent fund to the State Auditor, who shall draw his warrant on the State Treasurer for the amount of said claims and accounts, in favor of the persons to whom said claims and accounts so certified are due.

Approved December 5th, 1873.

No. 6.]   AN ACT

To suspend the sale of the 16th sections of lands in certain localities.

SECTION 1. *Be it enacted by the Board of Education of the State of Alabama*, That the sale of the sixteenth sections of lands in the following counties to-wit: Walker, Jefferson, DeKalb, Etowah, Shelby, Tuskaloosa, Bibb, Blount, Coosa, Cherokee, Winston, Fayette and Marion counties, be, and the same is hereby suspended until after the next session of the Board of Education.

SEC. 2. *Be it further enacted*, That all laws and parts of laws in conflict with the provisions of this act be, and the same are hereby repealed.

Approved Dec. 9, 1873.

No. 7.]   AN ACT

To repeal an act entitled an act to prevent the employment of teachers unless they can be promptly paid.

SECTION 1. *Be it enacted by the Board of Education of the State of Alabama*, That an act entitled an act to prevent the employment of teachers unless they can be promptly paid, approved December 14th, 1872, be, and the same is hereby repealed.

Approved December 6, 1873.

No. 8.]   AN ACT

Making election day a legal holiday.

SECTION 1. *Be it enacted by the Board of Education of the State of Alabama*, That the day of holding the general election be, and is hereby declared a legal holiday for teachers in free public schools.

SEC. 2. *Be it further enacted*, That this act shall take effect from and after its passage.

Approved December 5, 1873.

No. 9.]   AN ACT

To fix the length of a scholastic month.

SECTION 1. *Be it enacted by the Board of Education of the State of Alabama*, That from and after the passage of this act a scholastic month shall consist of twenty school days, and in computing the time, legal holidays and Saturdays shall not be included.

Twenty school days.

SEC. 2. *Be it further enacted*, That the Superintendent of Public Instruction shall prepare blanks for the reports of teachers and school officers, in accordance with the provision of section one (1) of this act.

SEC. 3. *Be it further enacted*, That all laws and parts of laws in conflict with the provisions of this act be, and the same are hereby repealed.

Approved December 6, 1873.

No. 10.]   AN ACT

To provide for filing and adjusting all claims against the Educational Department of the State, which accrued prior to the 1st of October, 1873.

SECTION 1. *Be it enacted by the Board of Education of the State of Alabama*, That all county superintendents, teachers of free public schools and all other parties who have claims unpaid against the educational department of the State of Alabama for services rendered prior to the first day of October, 1873, be, and hereby are required to forward to the superintendent of public instruction at Montgomery, Alabama, all such claims, properly made out, with the evidences of said indebtedness, and verified by affidavit of claimant, by the first day of October, 1874.

Claims to be filed with supt. of pub. inst'n.

SEC. 2. *Be it further enacted*, That all claims mentioned in section one of this act not presented as provided for in said section by the first day of October, 1874, shall be and are hereby barred from collection.

When barred.

SEC. 3. *Be it further enacted*, That it shall be the duty of the superintendent of public instruction of the State of Alabama, and he is hereby required to file in his office all the claims and evidences of the same forwarded under section one of this act, and to turn them over to the Committee on Finance and Claims, at the meeting of the Board of Education in the year 1874.

Duty of supt. of public inst'n.

SEC. 4. *Be it further enacted*, That each county superintendenent of education in this State be required to have this act posted up in three public places in each township of this county.

Duty of county superintendent

Approved December 5, 1873.

No. 11.]   AN ACT

To provide that tax collectors in certain contingencies shall perform the duties performed by and imposed on County Treasurers.

SECTION 1. *Be it enacted by the Board of Education of the State of Alabama,* That in the event the General Assembly should so amend an act entitled "An act to keep in each county in this State a proportionate share of the public school moneys," approved April 19, 1873, so as to relieve county treasurers of duties imposed by said act of the General Assembly, and impose the duties imposed by said act on tax collectors of each county instead of, as now on the county treasurers, then all the duties imposed on county treasurers by an act passed at the present session of the Board of Education entitled "An act to provide for the disbursement of school funds in the hands of county treasurers and State treasurer," shall be imposed on and performed by tax collectors of each county, and such tax collectors shall in that event receive the same compensation for such services as is now provided for county treasurers in said act passed at the present session of the Board of Education entitled "An act to provide for the disbursement of the school funds in the hands of county treasurers and State treasurer."

SEC. 2. *Be it further enacted,* That in the event the General Assembly shall repeal said act entitled "An act to keep in each county in this State a proportionate share of the public school money," approved April 19, 1873, then the tax collectors of each county shall do and perform all the duties imposed on county treasurers by an act passed at the present session of the Board of Education entitled "An act to provide for the disbursement of school funds in the hands of county treasurers and State treasurer," and said tax collectors shall also do and perform all duties imposed on county treasurers by said act of the General Assembly herein before mentioned, and said tax collector shall in that event receive the same compensation provided for county treasurers by said act passed at the present session of

[marginal notes] Contingency.   What duties.   Compensation.   How, if general assembly report.

the Board of Education entitled "an act to provide for the disbursement of school funds in the hands of county treasurers and State Treasurer."

Sec. 3. *Be it further enacted,* That all laws and parts of laws in conflict with this act be, and the same are hereby repealed.

Approved December 9, 1873.

No. 12.]   AN ACT

To provide for the disbursement of school funds in the hands of county treasurers and State Treasurer.

Section 1. *Be it enacted by the Board of Education of the State of Alabama,* That every county superintendent of education shall, at the close of each quarter, or as soon thereafter as possible, make a requisition in duplicate on the Superintendent of Public Instruction, for so much of the annual apportionment of the school fund to his county as is due for services authorized by law, and actually performed during said quarter, as shown by his quarterly report. The Superintendent of Public Instruction shall examine said requisitions, and if the requisitions do not exceed the amount due the several townships, he shall return one of said requisitions to the county superintendent of education approved; and if the requisition for any township is for an amount exceeding the amount due said township, he shall return it corrected and approved for an amount not in excess of the sum due said township. Each county superintendent of education shall be debited by the Superintendent of Public Instruction in his office with the amount of said requisition when approved.

Quarterly requisitions.

Duty of supt. of pub. instruct'n.

Sec. 2. *Be it further enacted,* That each county superintendent of education, on receipt of said approved requisition from the Superintendent of Public Instruction, shall draw warrants in favor of each teacher, or the person named in his requisition, for the amount due said teacher or other person for services authorized by law, and shall take receipts in

County supt. to draw warrants.

duplicate for such warrant or warrants from the same, and shall forward one of said receipts to the office of the Superintendent of Public Instruction, which shall be a voucher for the said county superintendent in his settlement of his accounts of said office.

SEC. 3. *Be it further enacted*, That the warrants drawn by the county superintendents of education upon the county treasurers in favor of teachers shall specify in what township, range and county said teacher rendered service, and out of the fund for what scholastic year and for what race they are to be paid. *What to be specified.*

SEC. 4. *Be it further enacted*, That the county treasurer of each county shall pay said warrants out of the school moneys in his hands in the order of their presentation. *County treasurer to pay said warrants.*

SEC. 5. *Be it further enacted*, That the county treasurer of each county, at the end of each quarter of the scholastic year, shall forward to the Superintendent of Public Instruction a statement of the amount of school money received from the tax collector, and the amount received from the State Treasurer, and each county treasurer shall be debited with said amount in the office of Superintendent of Public Instruction. Each county treasurer, at the end of each quarter, shall also forward to the Superintendent of Public Instruction all the warrants paid by him during the quarter, taking a receipt for the same, and said warrants shall be his vouchers for the disbursement of said school money. *County treasurer to forward statements.*

SEC. 6. *Be it further enacted*, That each county treasurer and county superintendent of education shall make an annual report, showing the operation of their respective offices, and the balance of school money unexpended belonging to their respective counties. Said reports shall be made in accordance with the Instructions of the Superintendent of Public Instruction. *Annual report of county superintendent.*

SEC. 7. *Be it further enacted*, That the State Auditor shall draw his warrant upon the State Treasurer for all amounts ordered by the Board of Education to be certified to the Auditor by the Superintendent of Public Instruction, and the State Treasurer shall pay said warrants. *Duty of State Auditor.*

Duty of supt. of pub. instruct'n. SEC. 8. *Be it further enacted*, That as soon as the Superintendent of Public Instruction shall make his supplemental apportionment provided in section fifth of an act of the General Assembly of Alabama, "To keep in each county of this State a proportionate share of the public school money," approved April 19th, 1873, he shall certify to the Auditor the amount due each county, and the Auditor shall draw his warrant on the State Treasurer for said sum in favor of each county treasurer, who shall draw and disburse said money in accordance with the provisions of this act.

Compensation of county supt. SEC. 9. *Be it further enacted*, That each county treasurer shall receive, as compensation for his services, one per centum of all school moneys received and disbursed by him under the provisions of this act, to be by him retained from said moneys so received and disbursed.

Books pento inspection. SEC. 10. *Be it further enacted*, That all books and papers of all county officers relating to free public school moneys and matters shall be open to inspection to all public school officers and teachers.

SEC. 11. *Be it further enacted*, That all laws and parts of laws in conflict with the provisions of this act be, and the same are hereby repealed.

Approved Dec. 9, 1873.

No. 13.]   AN ACT

To fix the times and places of the meetings of the Board of Regents of the State University.

Annual meeting. SECTION 1. *Be it enacted by the Board of Education of the State of Alabama,* That the Board of Regents of the State University shall meet annually at the State University, in the city of Tuskaloosa, on Monday before the first Wednesday in July: **Limit of session.** *Provided*, That the Board of Regents shall only draw per diem for the time they continue in session, not to exceed eight days.

Other meetings SEC. 2. *Be it further enacted*, That said Board may sit and transact business as such Board of Regents in the city of Montgomery during the sessions of the Board of Education.

Approved December 5, 1873.

No. 14.]   AN ACT

To prescribe and regulate the compensation of the members of the Board of Regents of the State University.

SECTION 1. *Be it enacted by the Board of Education of the State of Alabama*, That the members of the Board of Regents of the State University shall receive, while sitting as a Board of Regents, at the State University, as compensation, three dollars per diem while in session as such Board, and three dollars for every twenty miles traveled in going to and returning from the sessions of such Board, to be paid in national currency, or its equivalent, the distance to be determined by the affidavit of the respective members : *Provided*, They shall receive compensation for not more than eight days. Compensation at annual session. Proviso.

SEC. 2. *Be it further enacted*, That the per diem and mileage provided in the first section of this act shall be paid out of the University fund, upon the certificate of each member.

Approved December 5, 1873.

No. 15.]   AN ACT

To repeal an act entitled "An act to provide for the education of teachers of colored schools," approved December 20, A. D. 1871.

SECTION 1. *Be it enacted by the Board of Education of the State of Alabama*, That an act entitled "An act to provide for the education of teachers of colored schools," approved the 20th day of December, A. D. 1871, be, and the same is hereby repealed. Act repealed.

SEC. 2. *Be it further enacted*, That this act re-

When to take
effect. pealing the said act hereinbefore mentioned shall take effect and become operative on and after the first day of January, A. D. 1874.

Approved December 9, 1873.

No. 16.]   AN ACT

To amend the title and section 1 of an act entitled an act to establish a normal school at Florence, Alabama, for the education of white male teachers.

SECTION 1. *Be it enacted by the Board of Education of the State of Alabama*, That the title and section one (1) of the above recited act, which is in

Recitation. words and figures as follows, to-wit: "An act to establish a normal school at Florence, Alabama, for the education of white male teachers. Sec. 1. Be it enacted by the Board of Education of the State of Alabama, That if the president and trustees of the Florence Wesleyan University shall, by January 25, 1873, cause to be deposited with the State Superintendent of Public Instruction, a deed to the grounds and buildings of the Florence Wesleyan University, which deed shall be in favor of the Board of Education of the State of Alabama, then by the first day of October, 1873, and in consideration of the above named deed, there shall be permanently established in said Uuniversity buildings, a school for the education of white male teachers, which shall be taught on such conditions and under such restrictions as may be hereafter prescribed by law; *Provided*, That any pupil may be released from all obligations to teach by paying a moderate tuition for the time he may attend the school; *Provided further*, That as an additional consideration for the above named deed, that there shall be annually appropriated and set apart from and after the first day of October, 1873, at least five thou. sand dollars of the general educational fund of the State apportioned to the whites for the support and maintenance of said school; *Provided further*, That the grounds and buildings of the said Florence Wes-

leyan University shall remain in the possession, and
under the control of the said president and trustees,
free of all charges for rent or use until October 1st,
1873,"—be and the same is hereby amended so as to
read as follows, to-wit: An act to establish a normal Section as
school at Florence, Alabama, for the education of amended.
white male and female teachers. Section 1. Be it
enacted by the Board of Education of the State of
Alabama, That if the president and trustees of the
Florence Wesleyan University shall, by January
25th, 1873, cause to be deposited with the State Superintendent of Public Instruction a deed to the
grounds and buidings of the Florence Wesleyan
University, which deed shall be in favor of the Board
of Education of the State of Alabama, then by the
1st of October, 1873, and in consideration of the
above named deed, there shall be permanently established in said University buildings a school for the
education of white male and female teachers, which
teachers shall be taught on such conditions and under such restrictions as may be hereafter prescribed
by law; *Provided*, That any pupil may be released
from all obligations to teach by paying a moderate
tuition for the time he or she may attend the school;
Provided further, That as an additional consideration for the above named deed, that there shall be
annually appropriated and set apart, from and after
the 1st day of October, 1873, at least five thousand
dollars of the general educational fund of the State
apportioned to the whites for the support and maintenance of said school; *Provided further*, That the
grounds and buildings of the said Florence Wesleyan
University shall remain in the possession and under
the control of the said president and trustees, free
of all charges for rent or use until October 1, 1873.

SEC. 2. *Be it further enacted*, That the title and
section one of the above recited act, amended by
this act, and inconsistent with this amendment, is
hereby repealed.

Approved December 5, 1873.

No. 17.]   AN ACT

To establish a State normal school and university
for the education of colored teachers and students.

Contingency.

SECTION 1. *Be it enacted by the Board of Education of the State of Alabama*, That if the president and trustees of Lincoln School, located at Marion, shall place at the disposal of the Board of Education the school building for the use of said normal school and university, in accordance with articles of agreement that may be entered into between the president and trustees of said Lincoln School and the directors hereinafter named, there shall be State normal permanently established in said school building a school and university estab- State normal school and university for colored teachlished. ers and students, and said normal school and university shall be organized and operated under such restrictions and on such conditions as may be provided Provisos vided by law; *Provided*, That any pupil may be released from all obligation to teach by paying a moderate tuition for the time he may attend the normal school and university; *Provided*, That as an additional consideration for the above named use of said school building, there shall be annually appropriated and set apart, from and after the first day of January, 1874, two thousand dollars of the general educational fund apportioned to the colored race for the support and maintenance of said normal school and uiversity; *Provided*, That no portion of said sum shall be used for any other purpose whatever than the payment of teachers of said normal school.

Board of direc- SEC. 2. *Be it further enacted*, That Porter King, tors. John Harris, Joseph H. Speed, A. H. Curtis, John Dozier, J. H. Sears, John T. Foster, shall constitute a board of directors, which shall be known by the Name and style name and style of the Board of Directors of the State Normal School and University for the colored race, and said directors shall hold their office at the pleasure of the board, and shall receive no compensation.

Vacancy, how SEC. 3. *Be it further enacted*, That any vacancy filled. in said board of directors, caused by death, resignation, or otherwise, shall be filled by the remaining members, subject to the approval of the board.

SEC. 4. *Be it further enacted*, That the board of Meeting of the board. directors provided for in this act shall meet in the Lincoln School building, at Marion, at such time as may be designated by the Superintendent of Public Instruction not exceeding sixty days after the passage of this act, and at such other times and places as the board may appoint.

SEC. 5. *Be it further enacted*, That at their first Election of officers. meeting, the members of the board of directors shall choose one of their number as president of their own board, who shall not vote on any question except in case of a tie; and they shall elect a secretary and treasurer, and they shall take such bond from such treasurer as they shall deem sufficient and adequate to secure the faithful performance of his duties, at least double the amount that he may have in hand at any one time; said bond to be approved by the county superintendent and probate judge of Perry county, and a certified copy thereof shall be filed in the office of the Superintendent of Public Instruction. The secretary and treasurer shall be chosen annually, and shall hold their offices until their successors are elected and qualified.

SEC. 6. *Be it further enacted*, That the board shall, Disposal of moneys. under the restrictions and limitations of this act, direct the disposal of any and all moneys appropriated to said school, and shall prescribe the duties of the secretary and treasurer thereof.

SEC. 7. *Be it further enacted*, That it shall be Organization of the school and university. the duty of said board to organize a normal school upon the most approved plan, and in connection therewith a university department, in which such a course of instruction shall be established as shall meet the wants of the colored race, and provide for their education in the higher departments of learning, it being the intent and purpose of this act to provide for the liberal education of the colored race in the same manner as is already provided for the education of the white race in our university and colleges. The board of directors shall elect a president and a sufficient corps of instructors, who shall constitute the faculty of said normal school and university; and shall adopt such rules and regulations as may be necessary for the organization and

2

successful operation of said normal school and university, and the faculty shall have power to pass all rules and regulations necessary for the discipline of said institution, subject to the approval of the board of directors.

President to make an annual report.

SEC. 8. *Be it further enacted*, That the president of the board of directors shall make a full and complete annual report to the Board of Education, through its president, of the operations of said normal school and university, specifying the number of pupils, the number of professors or teachers, the amount of salary of each, the amount of money received and disbursed, and such other information as may be required by law.

Admission of applicants.

SEC. 9. *Be it further enacted*, That applicants for admission to said normal school and university shall be not less than fourteen years of age, and shall sustain a satisfactory examination in such studies as may be required by the faculty.

As to free tuition.

SEC. 10. *Be it further enacted*, That students shall be admitted from any portion of the State, and shall receive instruction free of charge for tuition, upon signing a written obligation to teach at least two years in the public schools of Alabama, and said obligation shall be filed in the office of Superintendent of Public Instruction : *Provided*, That

Proviso.

any student may be released from said obligation by paying such tuition as may be established by the board of directors.

State certificate of graduation.

SEC. 11. *Be it further enacted*, That upon the completion of the prescribed course of study in said normal school and university, and after sustaining a satisfactory examination, upon the recommendation of the president, approved by the board of directors, the Superintendent of Public Instruction shall issue a State certificate to the graduates of said normal school and university.

Public school in connection.

SEC. 12. *Be it further enacted*, That in connection with said normal school and university there may be established a public school or other school.

Money due, how to be obtained.

SEC. 13. *Be it further enacted*, That the money appropriated and due to said school shall be certified semi-annually by the Superintendent of Public Instruction to the State Auditor, upon application of the president of the board of directors, and the State

Auditor shall thereupon draw his warrant upon the State Treasurer in favor of the treasurer of said normal school and university, for the amount thus certified.

Sec. 14. *Be it further enacted*, That all laws and parts of laws in conflict with the provisions of this act be, and the same are hereby repealed.

Approved Dec. 6, 1873.

No. 18.]   **AN ACT**

To provide for a Colored Normal School at Huntsville, in Madison county, in the State of Alabama.

SECTION 1. *Be it enacted by the Board of Education of the State of Alabama*, That there shall be established at Huntsville, in this State, a normal school for the education of colored teachers. Pupils shall be admitted free of charge for tuition in said school, on giving an obligation in writing to teach in the free public schools of this State for two years after they become qualified. Said school shall not be begun or continued with a less number than twenty-five pupils, nor shall said school be taught for a less period than nine months in each year. *School authorized. Pupils free on condition. Term of session.*

SEC. 2. *Be it further enacted*, That there be, and is hereby, appropriated out of the general school fund appropriated to the colored children, the sum of one thousand dollars annually for the maintenance and support of said school, and that the apportionment of the general fund for the colored race shall be made to the different counties of this State after the deduction of said sum of one thousand dollars herein appropriated for said school at Huntsville. *Appropriation of fund.*

SEC. 3. *Be it further enacted*, That said school be under the direction, control and supervision of a board of three commissioners, who shall consist of the following persons, to-wit: James W. Steele, Joseph C. Bradley and Larkin Robinson, who may fill any vacancy that may occur in said board of commissioners. Said commissioners shall elect one *Board of commissioners.*

of their number chairman, who shall report annually to the Board of Education how many pupils have been in attendance at said school, what branches have been taught, and all other facts of interest and importance appertaining to said school, and said commissioners shall make a like report quarterly to the Superintendent of Public Instruction.

Make report.

SEC. 4. *Be it further enacted,* That the chairman of said board of commissioners shall give bond in double the amount of said appropriation to said school for the legal and faithful application of the sum appropriated by this act, said bond to be approved by the judge of probate of Madison county, and a certified copy thereof shall be sent to the Superintendent of Public Instruction to be filed in his office.

Chairman to give bond.

SEC. 5. *Be it further enacted,* That the chairman of said board of commissioners, after having given bond as hereinbefore prescribed, and said bond shall have been approved as herein provided, and a certified copy thereof filed in office of Superintendent of Public Instruction, shall present to the Superintendent of Public Instruction a requisition for the amount herein appropriated, namely, one thousand dollars, and the Superintendent of Public Instruction shall thereupon certify the said amount of one thousand dollars to the State Auditor, who shall draw his warrant for said sum on the State Treasurer, payable to said chairman of said board of commissioners, for the maintenance and support of said normal school.

Chairman to present a requisition.

SEC. 6. *Be it further enacted,* That all laws and parts of laws in conflict with the provisions of this act be, and the same are hereby repealed.

Approved Dec. 9, 1873.

No. 19.]   AN ACT

To ratify the removal of E. J. Morgan, and the appointment of P. D. Barker, as Superintendent of Education for the county of Dallas.

SECTION 1. *Be it enacted by the Board of Education of the State of Alabama*, That the removal by the Superintendent of Public Instruction, of Edward J. Morgan, from the office of superintendent of education for the county of Dallas, on account of drunkenness, on the first day of July, 1873, and the appointment by him of P. D. Barker to said office on the 9th day of July, 1873, be, and the same are hereby in all things ratified and confirmed, and that the said P. D. Barker be, and he is hereby declared to be the superintendent of education for the county of Dallas from the time of his appointment and qualification.

Approved Dec. 5, 1873.

No. 20.]   AN ACT

To legalize the action of the trustees of township 17, range 5, east, Marengo county in opening and operating the free public schools for the year 1872–73.

SECTION 1. *Be it enacted by the Board of Education of the State of Alabama*, That the action of trustees of township 17, range 5, east, Marengo county, in using the funds arising from the rent of the sixteenth section fund for the purpose of operating two colored schools on the basis of fifty dollars per month, for the salary of the teachers of the two colored schools, and sixty dollars per month for the salary of the teacher of the white school in said township during the year 1872–73, be, and the same is in all things ratified and confirmed.

SEC. 2. *Be it further enacted*, That the superintendent of Marengo county is hereby authorized and required to settle with said teachers in accordance with the provisions of section 1 (one) of this

Action legaliz'd

Basis of allowance.

County supt. to settle with the teachers.

Proviso.

act: *Provided*, That none of the surplus now on hand of said 16th section fund shall be used except the amount to be apportioned and belonging to the colored citizens of said township who sign a re-

Further provi-so.

linquishment to the same: *And, provided further*, That the amount so used shall be distributed *pro rata* among those who sign such relinquishment.

Approved December 6, 1873.

No. 21.]   AN ACT

To legalize the acts of the township trustees of township 5, of range 6, east, of Jackson county

SECTION 1. *Be it enacted by the Board of Education of the State of Alabama*, That the contract for drawing off a lake in section 16, of township 5, of range 6, east, in Jackson county, made and entered into April 1873, between Thomas B. Parks, and B. W. Tipton, trustees of said township and range, and one Nathaniel McCurdy, be, and the same is hereby ratified.

Approved Dec. 9, 1873.

No. 22.]   AN ACT

To authorize the Superintendent of Education of Perry county, to settle the accounts of Josephine Thomas, Mary F. Thomas, B. R. Thomas, C. J. Thomas, John Dozier, G. S. W. Lewis, Mrs. Matt. Smite, Mrs. Bethre Obering.

Authority con-ferred.

SECTION 1. *Be it enacted by the Board of Education of the State of Alabama*, That the superintendent of education of Perry county is hereby authorized and required to ascertain the amounts due Josephine Thomas, Mary F. Thomas, B. R. Thomas, C. J. Thomas, John Dozier, G. S. W. Lewis, Mrs. Matt. Smith, Mrs. Bethre Obering, for services rendered in the free public school in accordance with law, in the county of Perry, and he shall pay the amounts due said persons above named *Out of funds of* out of any funds for the year 1871, due the respect- *1871.* ive townships in which they taught.

Approved December 9, 1873.

No. 23.]   AN ACT

To pay Jas. L. Tait, for services rendered in examining the mineral sixteenth sections.

SECTION 1. *Be it enacted by the Board of Education of the State of Alabama*, That the sum of *Appropriation* five hundred dollars be, and the same is hereby ap- *of $500.* propriated out of any unexpended money belonging to the school fund or so much thereof is necessary, to pay Jas. L. Tait for services rendered in pursuance of an order of this Board in examining mineral sixteenth sections.

SEC. 2. *Be it further enacted*, That the Superintendent of Public Instruction, is hereby authorized and required to examine the claim of same Jas. L. Tait, and he shall certify the amount due him for said services specified in section one of this act, to the Auditor, who shall draw his warrant for said amount so certified upon the Treasurer, who shall pay the warrant out of the money appropriated in section one (1) of this act.

Approved December 9, 1873.

No. 24.]   AN ACT

For the relief of the widow of Bryce M. Almond.

SECTION 1. *Be it enacted by the Board of Education of the State of Alabama*, That the county *Authority con* superintendent of education of Marengo county, is *ferred.* hereby authorized and required to pay to the widow of Bryce M. Almond, the amount due said Bryce M. Almond, deceased, for services rendered as teacher of free public colored school No. 1, in township 17, range 4, east, as shown by his reports, and that the receipt of the widow of said Bryce M. Almond, for the money paid to her and due said Bryce M. Almond, deceased, shall be a legal voucher to the county superintendent of education of Marengo county, in his settlement of his accounts with the Superintendent of Public Instruction.

Approved December 9, 1873.

No. 25.]   AN ACT

For the relief of Mrs. Georgia Sims, of Chambers county.

SECTION 1. *Be it enacted by the Board of Education of the State of Alabama,* That T. W. Green, county superintendent of education for Chambers county be, and the same is hereby instructed to pay to Miss Georgia Sims, the sum of sixty dollars, for services rendered as teacher in the year 1872, out of any unexpended funds in his hands for said year belonging to township twenty, and range twenty-seven of Chambers county.

Authority to county supt.

Approved Dec. 6, 1873.

No. 26.]   AN ACT

To provide for the relief of Miss D. W. Caller.

SECTION 1. *Be it enacted by the Board of Education of the State of Alabama,* That the superintendent of education for the county of Clarke, be, and he is hereby instructed to pay out of any unexpended school funds belonging to township 6, range 4, east, of said county for the year 1872, the claim of Miss D. W. Caller, for the sum of eighty dollars, for services rendered by her as teacher in the year 1872.

Authority to county supt.

Approved December 5, 1873.

No. 27.]   AN ACT

For the relief of Miss V. C. Law, of Clarke county.

SECTION 1. *Be it enacted, by the Board of Ed-* Authority to
ucation of the State of Alabama, That the su- county supt.
perintendent of education of Clarke county, be, and
he is hereby instructed to pay the claim of Miss V.
C. Law, for the sum of sixty-four dollars for services rendered as teacher during the first term of
scholastic year 1873, before the public schools of
said year were ordered closed, out of any unexpended funds due township eleven (11), range one (1)
west, of said county for the year 1873.

Approved December 5, 1873.

No. 28.]   AN ACT

For the relief of W. J. Johnson, of township 12,
range 2, east, Clarke county.

SECTION 1. *Be it enacted by the Board of Ed-* Authority to
ucation of the State of Alabama, That the super- county supt.
intendent of education for Clarke county, be, and
he is hereby instructed to pay out of any unexpended funds due township 12, range 2, east, of
said county for the year 1873, the claim of W. J.
Johnson, for forty dollars for services as teacher,
rendered during said scholastic year before the
public schools of said year were closed.

Approved December 5, 1873.

INDEX.

31